The Amazing Zoo

H. B. Gilmour
Pictures by Nate Evans

Aladdin Paperbacks

Aladdin Paperbacks
An imprint of Simon & Schuster Children's Publishing Division
1230 Avenue of the Americas
New York, New York 10020
All rights reserved including the right of reproduction in whole or in part in any form.
First Aladdin Paperbacks edition, April 1996
Designed by Chani Yammer and Nancy Widdows
The text of this book was set in 17 point Syntax.
Manufactured in the United States of America
10 9 8 7 6 5 4 3 2 1
ISBN: 0-689-80421-0

Today my brother Rondo's class is going to the zoo.
I want to go, too.

But while Rondo is visiting the monkeys and the giraffes, I'll be having a snack and taking a nap at Ms. Melody's Little Blue Day Care.

It isn't fair!

I don't want to be in day care today. What I really, really, really want to do is . . .

get splashed by a seal or shake hands with a kangaroo or share a bag of peanuts with an elephant.

I tell Ms. Melody how I feel. Then we have a great idea.
We can make our own zoo!

We hand out scissors and paints and paste.

We draw whiskers and ears and tails and manes.

Then we try on our masks.

It's amazing, all right. We point at each other and giggle and laugh.

Even Riff and Lindi join in. Lindi's a penguin.
She wobbles when she walks.

Riff roars like a lion. *R-R-Roar!* He's the king of the cats.

I scratch like a monkey. I swing from a tree.

Nobody is a better monkey than me!

At naptime I dream Rondo visits our zoo. He says, "Cool!"

I like it, too!

When we wake up, it's snack time. There are animal crackers to eat with our milk and our juice!

Guess what we do next? It's the most fun of all. We have a zoo parade.

We growl and hiss and roar and hoot and hop and slither and gallop and soar. All our friends wave and cheer.

When I get home, Rondo is there.

He tells me how much fun it was seeing all the animals. Then he asks, "Allegra, what did *you* do today?"

We had fun, too. We made our *own* zoo!